LOUD SNOW

LOUD SNOW

STORIES

Leah Browning

Silent Station Press

Published in the United States of America
by Silent Station Press.

Cover painting: *Phoenix and Sun*
by Ito Jakuchu

Publisher's Cataloging-in-Publication Data

Browning, Leah
Loud snow: stories / Leah Browning
ISBN 978-0-578-37677-6
Short stories, American. | Short stories
(single author). | Domestic fiction.

Contents

LOUD SNOW

Role-Play

———————

Harriet and Ralph were halfway to Felton when Ralph told her that they were on their way to a Civil War reenactment. The traffic, which had all but stopped, started moving again, and Harriet was able to get away with saying, "We are?" in a way that she hoped sounded more enthusiastic than she felt. It was the first blind date she'd ever been on, and she wasn't sure how these things were supposed to go.

Their mutual friend, the one who had set them up, was a high school history teacher. Somehow Ralph must have gotten the idea that Harriet was as well. No matter. She studied the scenery, determined to be a good sport.

It was Memorial Day weekend, and the other cars were packed with families on their way to the beach. As soon as they'd gotten on the road, the thought had unspooled: a lazy day walking on the shore, a bucketful of seashells, white wine and oysters for dinner.

On the phone, when they'd arranged the date, she'd asked where he wanted to go, and Ralph had said that he wanted to surprise her. She hated surprises. He sounded so eager, though, that she couldn't bear to say so. It had been a long time since someone had wanted to please her.

The parking lot was unpaved, and once they were outside the car they could hear cannons in the distance. Nearby, a toddler was crying and clinging to his mother. Harriet could feel her heart beat faster. Ralph took her arm as they picked their way through the dirt and stones toward the battleground. He wasn't her type. She'd known that immediately. But maybe they could be friends? There was something comfortable about him. Reassuring.

They watched the soldiers shoot each other and fall to the ground. "Don't worry," a woman said to the younger of two little girls. "He's not really dead. This is like a play."

After the battle, Ralph bought Harriet an oversized hot dog and a bag of chips, and they ate at a picnic table while a band played country music. Before they went on the train, Harriet bought them ice cream.

Most of the souvenir shops and concession stands were closing by the time they got back. A man was sweeping with a long-handled broom. Ralph drove her back to his place. It was dusk and the traffic was slow again, but Harriet didn't mind. She looked out the window.

Earlier, a woman role-playing a nurse had lifted her props off a table one by one, demonstrating the use of each rudimentary medical tool. She said that she only had two dresses, and they were both dark to hide spilled blood. On the train, the leaves of the trees had shone in the sunlight. A branch had whipped in under the canopy and almost knocked someone over. As the train continued around a curve, the branch snapped.

Ralph put the kettle on for tea. Harriet sat on the couch, looking around at his living room.

She was the one who brought up chickens, saying that she wanted to keep some when she retired, and Ralph agreed. His sister, Beverly, lived in Arizona with her five children and three chickens that they kept in the back yard. Two of the chickens often picked on the third, Ralph said, and that was why he wanted an even number.

His sister had been a surprise baby, he said, born the fall he went to college.

So in many ways, though they were siblings, he had been an only child, and then she had been.

Their parents were dead now. Every year, Ralph visited Beverly in Tucson for a week or two at a time. On one of the bookshelves in the living room, he had a shelf of photographs, and he pointed out several of his sister and brother-in-law and the children. Sometimes they would go in the back yard, where even in the summer it was cool in the shade of an enormous mesquite tree, and gather eggs from the henhouse. Beverly would boil them and make egg salad sandwiches for lunch.

What else do you want? Ralph asked.

A pair of goats, Harriet said. Someone she knew had had one when she was a child, and she still re-membered learning how to milk it. A vegetable garden. And maybe . . . She hesitated, blushing, but then she didn't know why. Maybe honeybees.

Ralph nodded. He was smiling. From the other room, Harriet heard the whistle of the teakettle.

Elise in Italy

It's late, but she can't sleep. Instead, she's lying in bed in her hotel room watching a movie on MTV. It's *Footloose*, but dubbed into Italian, so she can only understand a word here or there. She's at the point where John Lithgow stops the townspeople from burning the books. He gives an impassioned speech, shaming them just enough that he can hand the books back and send everybody home.

It's been several years since Elise has seen the entire movie, but she's found it often enough while flipping channels at home that she knows the story backwards and forwards. The preacher father, the rebellious daughter. She was that kind of daughter herself, at one time.

They're already past the scene where the girl's boyfriend slaps her and says, "You'll wrap those skinny legs around anyone." Or, at least, that's the way Elise remembers it. She hates that part, and she's always relieved when she watches the movie on American cable and it's been edited out.

Now, to her surprise, she wants to see it—at least, to see the crescendo of anger and sexual jealousy filtered through this particular lens—to see what Italians make of the moment when the daughter's boyfriend is sure about Ren. The first time Elise was in Italy, she saw a bus driver who had narrowly avoided a collision with a small car lean out the window of his bus to scream and wave his arms at the other driver. No one else seemed to find this remarkable. Then both men finished screaming and drove away.

It's only been two days, but on this trip, Elise hasn't left the hotel since she checked in. It's all she can do to pull herself together and go downstairs for meals. *Ciao. Buongiorno.* It's been so long since she's been to Italy that she had to look up the word "breakfast" when she got back up to the room. She can't remember how to communicate. The best she can do is offer a weak smile and say *grazie*, but it is all right. In the hotel restaurant, they smile back. They accept her limitations.

Kenny Loggins is singing. *Now I gotta cut loose. Footloose. Kick off your Sunday shoes.* The preacher is outside with his wife. She has already spoken in her soft voice and pressed up against him in the dark. The music from the television suddenly seems too loud.

In the middle of the night, Elise wakes and can't go back to sleep. She stands at the window in a white nightgown and looks outside. Under the darkness there are churches and piazzas that have been here for hundreds of years. One afternoon, she sat at a table in an outdoor square and ate a green salad with lemon while the voice of a woman singing opera floated from the upper windows of a neighboring school. At night, though, alone in this hotel room, Elise could be anywhere. If she didn't know better, she might think she was back in Ohio right now.

She walks away from the window, touching everything in the dark. Her suitcase, the tabletop, the back of a chair. The smooth gray floor is cold on her bare feet. It's a business hotel, with rooms that are clean and quiet. There's the flat-screen TV behind her. White pillowcases and a white coverlet on the bed.

Elise picks up a hotel pen and turns on the little desk lamp. She takes out a piece of paper. *Dear Michael.*

The therapist has told her that it might help to write him a letter.

She stares at the wall. *On my way here, I saw two young men carrying a mattress*, she thinks. *I asked the driver to stop the car. I turned to ask where you thought they were going, but you weren't there.*

For several blocks down Via Genova, they carried it between them—a small mattress, suitable for a child. They walked slowly. It was dusk. A man on a bicycle rode past, illuminating them briefly with his headlamp. From the opposite direction, a teenage girl passed them with a giant stuffed bear clutched against her stomach. Inside a salon, a woman lay with her head in a basin while another woman rinsed purple foam out of her hair. Next door to the salon was a laundromat with wedding dresses in the window.

In the adjoining hotel room, someone opens and closes the closet doors.

What is this person doing in the middle of the night?

At last, Elise puts the pen down and turns off the light.

She's almost asleep when the telephone rings. Her heart is beating fast when she picks it up and says hello. There's no one on the other end. She can hear a series of tones. A mistake, perhaps? Or not. She hangs up the phone and lies still, waiting for another signal. An alarm, a knock at the door. A message of some kind, telling her what to do next.

Elise in Austria

She's lying in a hotel room in Vienna watching *The King of Queens* dubbed into German. It's the episode where Carrie is in her home office upstairs, busy for days on end with a big project, and Holly the dog walker—who usually "walks" Carrie's dad—starts cooking for Doug.

Elise doesn't speak German, but the body language is unmistakable. The dog walker spoils him, making elaborate pancake breakfasts. She catches him drinking straight from the orange juice. When he offers a sheepish apology, she says something that Elise doesn't understand, though she seems to be urging him to do something; he grins and drinks the rest of the juice in one long swallow. Admiringly, she hands him a dollar.

It's as if Doug has two wives, and the best of both. Carrie asks him to sleep with her—to relax her, it seems, or to clear her head—and afterwards, as they leave the bedroom—Doug smiling, zipping up the long neck of his pullover sweater, Carrie calling "Danke" as she goes back to her home office to resume her work—he walks downstairs and finds Holly in the kitchen, just finishing frosting a chocolate cake.

Back at home, Elise has seen this episode in English, and she turns the television off before the fantasy starts to unravel.

The next day, she wakes up long past the alarm. She slept terribly the night before, still jet-lagged though she's been in Europe for days now. She eats a late breakfast in the hotel restaurant and goes outside, rushing past the gardens of Hofburg Palace.

There is no time to see anything now. She has paid €5 for a standing room ticket to hear the Vienna Philharmonic, but she gets lost on the way to the ticket office and is almost late for the concert.

The room is crowded, and Elise regrets the standing room ticket almost immediately. She wore running shoes under her dress, thinking that would help, but it's no use. During the intermission, a group of students moves to the back of the room, where they sit on the floor along the mirrored wall. An older woman trips over one of their legs as she crosses the room from one side to the other. A tall, elegant-looking man catches the woman and narrowly prevents her from falling, but she jerks her arm away from him. She snaps at the man in German, and he turns on the students. "This is a standing room," he says angrily in

English. The students say nothing that Elise can hear. They have stopped taking photos of each other against the backdrop of the Golden Hall and are texting and listening to music on their headphones.

By the time the concert is over, it is already dark outside. Instead of going straight back to the hotel, Elise stops at the Christmas Market on the Rathaus-platz, the square in front of the town hall. The weather was milder in Italy, and she's forgotten her gloves, but she buys a brat with mild German mustard and a mug of hot spiked punch and finds an empty spot on one of the benches behind the booths of candy and Christmas ornaments.

Elise notices a young boy skulking around the benches, waiting for anyone who is too drunk or distracted to return his mug and collect the €3 deposit. Before she even finishes her brat, Elise calculates that the boy has made at least €12 on mugs.

On her way to the hotel, as she's leaving the grounds of the Christkindlmarkt, Elise walks past a little building where she can hear a recording of a man. It startles her: this deep, booming voice reading aloud in German. Whole families walk up and lean toward the light from the windows. Inside, an animatronic bear as big as a grown man is sitting in a chair, reading a book of fairy tales to an odd assortment of other, much smaller animals that have been arranged throughout the room.

The scene should be charming, but instead Elise finds it creepy. The recording of the voice, the misfit animals.

She backs away from the building. It's windy. Her face and neck are cold and her feet ache. Still, for the first time in months, she feels grateful to be alive.

As she's falling asleep that night, Elise thinks of Doug Heffernan, walking into his kitchen and finding, unexpectedly, a chocolate cake.

Elise in Croatia

Kamelija meets her at the little airport in Zagreb. She is driving a beat-up VW Passat with no driver's side mirror. They squeeze Elise's suitcase and bag into the trunk, next to the engine.

The apartment is up a steep flight of stairs followed by a short elevator ride. Inside, the commode is in its own little room, just off the front door. The sink, a half-size bathtub, and a tiny washing machine are down the hall.

For dinner, Kamelija stands at the stove and fries sardines, big ones, nothing like the bite-sized fish Elise would find in small silver tins in the grocery store at home. On the other burner, Kamelija cooks chunks of potato in a bath of butter and milk and fresh herbs. She serves the fish and potatoes with wine and a salad of lettuce, tomatoes, and sautéed red bell peppers with chunks of feta and green olives and pumpkinseed oil, and crème brûlée for dessert.

Elise has only known Kamelija for six months. They were thrown together at a conference, the only two women in their group. Kamelija is self-conscious about her spoken English but more confident in writing. "When you are in Europe, you must visit," she told Elise. "I will take care of you."

They sit in the living room after dinner. Kamelija has collected miniatures from all over the world, and she keeps them in display cases and scattered around the room on tables and bookshelves. She points out a chain of carved elephants, a painting the size of Elise's thumb.

Kamelija has brought in bowls of fruit and chocolate, and they drink black wine. White wine, Kamelija told

Elise at dinner, has the same meaning in Croatia. Red wine, though, is what Elise would call rosé back in the United States, and "black wine" is an American red. After a couple of glasses, these distinctions no longer seem notable.

That night, Elise has trouble sleeping. Kamelija has made up a bed for her on the couch. Outside, it is raining lightly, and Elise tiptoes over to the window. Kamelija's bedroom is right next door, and she doesn't want to disturb her.

As Elise returns to the couch, her slippers brushing against the rug, the television suddenly flickers on. The connection is bad—it's nothing more than loud snow. There are two remotes on the coffee table, but neither seems to control the TV. Elise stares at the gray screen. This feels like a message, some ghostly communication. Her heart is beating too fast. It takes her a few seconds to snap out of it. She pokes the power button on the front of the screen, and the light fades. Elise sits on the edge of the couch, breathing hard, shaken.

In the morning, she asks Kamelija if the television woke her, but she shakes her head no. Kamelija rose early; she has already laid out a breakfast of homemade bread, slices of meat and cheese, fresh apricot marmalade, and strong black coffee.

After they have eaten, Kamelija shows Elise around the city. They start near the communist-era gray cinderblock buildings and continue past the older, more ornate shops and churches. At the top of the hill, overlooking the city, Kamelija buys Elise a paper cone of hot chestnuts from a street vendor. They walk back down on a steep, winding path lined with trees and lanterns.

Elise is cold as they walk back. It is

5 degrees Celsius and the wind is picking up. She thinks longingly of a pair of lined gloves on a shelf in her closet at home. On their way toward the hill, they already passed the fishmongers and piles of fruit at the daily farmer's market, but they are returning from a different direction, walking past the flower stalls. Kamelija pauses only briefly in front of the roses and birds of paradise.

They cut through an octagon-shaped building with an ornate stained-glass panel in the ceiling. Inside, though, out of the wind, they find a photo shoot in progress. A woman, bent at the waist, has on her back a young white cat wearing a harness and leash. A second woman is waving a feather toy hanging from a stick, trying unsuccessfully to turn the cat's attention toward a man with his face painted to look like a cat.

When they get back outside, Kamelija says that it is time to stop for first aid. Elise shakes her head, uncomprehending. Kamelija points toward a nearby building and draws a plus sign in the air in front of her. It takes Elise a moment to realize that Kamelija is making a joke. She takes Elise into a coffee shop and orders them each a slice of chocolate cake and a cup of hot tea.

It's late afternoon, and the sun is already low in the sky by the time they leave. They pass by a row of shops. One window has a sign in English, and Elise stops to read it. *Museum of Broken Relationships*. A mistranslation, she thinks.

Kamelija has also stopped.

"What does this mean?" Elise asks, pointing.

"It is the museum," Kamelija says. When Elise gives her a questioning look, she nods. Then, "Do you want to go inside?"

They have never spoken about anyone in their personal lives outside of their parents, siblings, and various friends. Elise doesn't want to stir anything up. She is curious, though, and Kamelija seems untroubled by the idea. Elise tries to hand her 50 kuna, but Kamelija waves the money away and pays the admission fee herself.

Inside, they don't stay together. Elise walks slowly past the exhibits. It's a relief to be here with someone who never knew Michael, who doesn't ask any questions.

Just before she left for Europe, Elise received a note from a university professor. The woman had interviewed Michael not long before his death, and she sent her condolences. "I'll send you a copy of the interview after its publication," the professor wrote. "I'm sure you'll want to see it."

One of the items on display is a white toaster. The submission is from someone in Denver, Colorado, who wrote, "When I moved out, and across the country, I took the toaster. That'll show you. How are you going to toast anything now?"

She is still looking at this card when Kamelija reappears.

"Elise," she says, and Elise looks up.

"You are hungry," Kamelija says. "Let's go."

She waves her hand in the direction of the front door, the world outside. She starts walking and looks back, gesturing again. "Come. Elise, come."

Elise hesitates. She looks back at the white toaster. She has to resist the urge to put her hand on the pedestal to ground herself. She wants something to hold on to.

Kamelija is waiting. "Come," she says again. Elise closes her eyes for a second, and then she turns and follows Kamelija into the future.

Armie

For years, Roy had been drawing a popular comic strip for a local newspaper. His girlfriend wanted to get married and buy a house near the beach. He told her: Give me one year. If it's not syndicated by then, I'll quit drawing and go back to practicing law.

At the end of the year, the comic was still not in syndication. He marked the last X on the calendar in his desk drawer. The next morning, he called and made an appointment at his old firm. On the way to the meeting, he bumped into one of his former colleagues in the parking lot. See you finally gave up, the shithead said, smirking.

He'd made partner and bought a gold Maserati since Roy had left.

So Roy went back to work. The firm was doing well, but they still lowballed him on the salary. He'd gone back for a 5K pay cut.

Still, he thought, his girlfriend had waited long enough. He raided his savings and bought her a diamond. On their anniversary, they drove down to the beach. He took her to a restaurant with a view of the water, and after dessert, he got down on one knee.

They had a simple ceremony and bought the beach house a year later. It was just a little one, though, for weekends, and it turned out that once he was back in the thick of things, he rarely had time to go out there. They ended up selling it at a loss, but by that time, they were happy to get rid of it. What had looked charming and weathered at sunset with a realtor was just plain shabby in broad daylight. They were getting killed on the maintenance.

And they needed the money, because she kept getting pregnant and had already quit her job after the first baby. Don't you know how these things happen? his brother asked when she showed up in a maternity shirt only six months after the third one was born. At night, after tucking the kids into bed, sometimes they split a bottle of wine and watched a movie. More often, she fell asleep at eight and he retreated to his home office.

Do you still do your little drawings? his grandmother asks him one year at Thanksgiving. When he shakes his head mutely, she pats his hand and says, Don't worry. You can always start again. You have all the time in the world. He's a fifty-year-old man. She's in her early nineties.

His wife is on the other side of the table, wearing a baggy sweater and a pair of baggy slacks. One of the younger kids is making a mess with his mashed potatoes. Their older daughter is a teenager now and she doesn't want anything to do with this. She's slumped down in her chair, sullenly pushing carrot coins across her otherwise empty plate. Depending on the day, she's a vegetarian or a vegan. On the day they planned the meal, vegetarian. Today, vegan. Go figure. There isn't a single item on the table that hasn't been slathered with at least two sticks of butter.

He tries to catch her eye. He wants to smile at her. He wants to be a better father than his father was. She looks away, crossing her arms pointedly.

Roy finishes his wine and gets up to refill the glass. He's stumbling a little but how the hell else is he supposed to make it through this? Every year is the same. The same turkey, the same good china, some spoiled brat giving him the stink eye.

His favorite character in his comic strip was a fat little Texas armadillo with a perpetual glass of scotch and a sharp tongue. Sometimes, especially when Roy's been drinking, he imagines what the armadillo would say to him, if he could see the situation Roy has gotten himself into. Slogging through his work, washing the car, paying the neighbor's kid $15 a week to drag a mower across the front lawn for five minutes and then pose in front of Roy's teenage daughter's bedroom, flexing his muscles and fluffing his mullet.

Standing in line at the grocery store, going on one vacation a year, going through the motions with this blah blah blah life—but what should he have done? What would have happened? He would have been poor and probably alone, because she wouldn't have stuck it out with him.

He's standing at the kitchen island fumbling with the corkscrew, and somehow he drops the bottle of wine on the floor. It's a red, a Bordeaux something—his eyes are too tired to focus and the bottle is broken. The trash under the sink is already full. Still, he gets down on his knees, trying to sop up wine and broken glass with a wad of paper towels.

He can feel the armadillo, nearby, watching.

What would you have done instead, he wants to ask, but as always, he is afraid to hear the response.

Shame

On her way out of the parking lot, Janine hit a parked car. She got out and leaned down, inspecting the damage. One of the back taillights was crushed.

It was Halloween. That morning, she'd dressed up as a German beer maid. The full white blouse was gathered around her midsection by a black corset-style bodice with shoulder straps and front laces, and the green skirt fell just above her knees.

She straightened. In the back seat of her car, the two little girls were also wearing costumes: Raggedy Ann, with red yarn for hair, and a butterfly with glittery makeup on her face and hands.

"Stay here," Jan said, and went back into the bank. "Does anyone own a beige Toyota?" they could see her asking at the counter.

It was a long strip mall. She walked from store to store, asking.

"Does anyone want me?" she was saying.

She was always making mistakes, doing the wrong thing, sending the wrong item on the wrong day. Once, when Janine overslept, the butterfly made her own lunch and the principal called home. A sharp little metal crown—part of a prize or a broken piece of a toy—was embedded in the apple she'd packed. It had been there so long that the flesh had rotted around it. A slice of bread that she'd used for her sandwich had soft spots of mold.

Still, Jan went on trying to make it work, opening the next door, looking for the one person who would say yes.

I watched her walk toward the car. I'd already gotten the baby out of his car seat and I held him in my lap. He had pulled off the black headband with the cat ears. He was fussing, chewing on his fist. My little sisters kicked the back of my seat. Kick. Kick.

She leaned in the open car window. "Sorry, Josie," she said. "Just a couple more minutes." There was a slick glaze of sweat on her forehead.

The baby began to wail, reaching for her. "As soon as we get home, I'll get you a bottle," she said, and patted his hand.

A few people were emerging from the shops, looking at us curiously.

She turned and walked toward them. They were the businessmen in the bar, loosening their ties and waiting for a drink. The green skirt twirled above the long white lengths of her calves, the soft insides of her knees.

I looked away, but still, I could hear her voice, rising.

From a Distance, It Always Sounds Like Begging

In her bedroom, Janine is on the phone. She's being so loud that I'm afraid she's going to wake the baby again.

Down the hall, my little sisters are asleep. The younger one still sucks her thumb, and at night, when she has a bad dream, she cries and crawls into bed with me.

Earlier, Janine was on the phone with the landlord, pacing back and forth across the living room as she tried to sweet-talk him into another week, another two weeks, because she can't pay the rent on time, but she's got half of it, she's got almost half of it and she just needs a little more time.

She was already in her nightgown—a short one, white eyelet with a pale pink ribbon laced through the bodice—and she paused in front of the mirror, closing her eyes as she said wearily, "I know, I'm sorry. I'll bring you a check as soon as I can."

Now, in the bedroom, her voice rises as she says, "But what'll we do for groceries? Please, I need it."

On the nights she's been drinking, she's more likely to cry when she talks to him, but tonight she's not slurring her words or bumping into the dresser across from her bed.

I have a chemistry test in the morning, and I try to visualize the periodic table. I can't get Jan to call me in again; I've missed too much school as it is.

When the lady from the attendance office called the apartment, she didn't ask to speak to Janine, just launched right in, saying, "Miss Smith, your daughter," blah blah blah.

When she got done, I said, "It's Mrs. Lenox now," like a queen, because this was when things were still good and I was starting to think that it might work out.

There was a long pause. "Congratulations," the lady said, finally. "You should come in and update Josie's file," but we both knew she'd never make it into the office, and then it didn't really matter anymore anyway.

"I don't know what you expect me to do," Jan says now. I'm so tired that the numbers on my clock radio are shimmering in the dark. "No, don't hang up!" she says. "We need to figure something out!"

He must have hung up because I can hear the frantic sound of the numbers as she tries to call him back. "Dammit," she says. "Dammit."

In the morning, I know, her eyes will be swollen as she stands at the counter, shoving bologna sandwiches into waxed paper bags for the little girls' lunches.

I can hear the baby start up.

The door of her bedroom swings open. If she's not careful, she's going to wake the little girls. Her bare feet make the faintest sound as she walks across the floor, hesitating only briefly before she turns the knob. She kneels next to my bed.

"Josie, please," she says, and I get up and go into her bedroom. The baby is lying in the crib, flailing his arms.

I pick him up and hold him against my shoulder, letting him sob for a moment into my neck. He grasps the soft fabric of my shirt and twists it in his hands.

"It'll be all right," I say. I hold him close and pat his back, and take him to the kitchen to warm a bottle.

Josephine,
Planting Sunflowers

In an hour, more or less, Janine will drive up the long slant of the driveway in that old brown Datsun she has. I haven't seen her in six months. It was winter then. One morning, we woke up and the snowdrifts were piled so high outside her front door that we weren't able to open it.

Now, I'm standing in the garden, sweating in a tank top and shorts. It's not that I'm trying to impress her exactly, but I do want her to see me like this: tan and muscular, my hair in a thick braid down my back. More and more, I feel that anything could happen between this visit and the next time I see her. I turned forty this year, and at my annual appointment, when I mentioned that I'd been waking up in pain, the doctor said, "It's just a downhill slide from here."

Yet Janine, who is in her late fifties, has a new boyfriend. She didn't mention him over the phone, so I only know what I've heard secondhand, from my younger sisters. They both live on the east coast now, with their matching husbands, in their matching condos. One has two girls, the other two boys, and they each have a small white Bichon Frise that yaps around the house when I visit.

They still talk about Janine like she's in her twenties, in the midst of one divorce or another. She spent years of our childhood crying over the husband who turned out to be a drunk, the boyfriend who had a whole other family in a better part of town.

But this was all so long ago. No matter what happened, Janine went on waking up. She stood at the kitchen counter mixing pancake batter in her old red silk kimono. After school and on weekends, she put on eye makeup and dropped the girls at the neighbor's and went to work while I stayed home with our baby brother.

There were nights when she had to call one of her parents and ask for money, laughing, saying she preferred candlelight but the kids were spoiled and wanted electricity. There was a brittle edge that I sometimes thought only I could hear.

We got most of our clothes at yard sales, and if my little sisters complained, Janine said, "You know what they say about beggars and choosers."

Recently, I found an old letter from Janine. "Josie," it began, but I found that I didn't want to read the rest. Sometimes the past is just the past. In large, looping letters, she had written "All my love, Mom" at the bottom of the page. I folded it up and placed it back in the drawer.

I've taken the week off work. Janine and I are planning to spend a few days driving down the coast. Tonight, though, I'm going to open a bottle of red wine and cook for her. I have popcorn and a stack of DVDs. It'll be just the two of us again.

I stand, shading my eyes against the sun. Any minute now, I'll look down the hill and see Janine's little brown Datsun working its way up the driveway toward me.

The Third of Three Stories About Men and Animals

Mark and his boyfriend were driving down to Florida when the car broke down. They'd bought tickets for a sunset dinner cruise that weekend. Mark's mother was a retired travel agent, and she had always loved these excursions: an elaborate dinner, a glass of champagne, an hour or two of music and dancing. She was almost eighty and still loved to kick up her heels.

They called her from the side of the road while they waited for a tow truck. "I don't know if we're going to make it there by tonight," Mark said. He was sweating, and the phone stuck to his cheek.

He hung up and sighed. It was midafternoon on a workday. There were no other cars in sight. Best-case scenario, they'd be cooling their heels—only figuratively speaking, of course—for another half-hour.

"Look," his boyfriend said, pointing. On the other side of the wire fence, in the shade of a large tree, were three ostriches.

One of the birds marched toward the fence, shooting hostile looks in the men's direction. He paused, bobbing his neck up and down, and then flapped his enormous wings threateningly.

"We're bothering them," Mark's boyfriend said.

"Well, what are we supposed to do?" Mark asked. "We can't leave the car." Somehow they'd managed to grind to a halt next to an ostrich farm. Next thing they knew, an angry ostrich farmer would stride out, shaking a meaty fist and yelling at them to get off his property.

(But the road was public property, wasn't it? Mark imagined making this argument but wasn't sure whether the farmer would accept it or not. He was only a caricature of a farmer, a jean-overall-wearing idea that Mark had gotten from cartoons and movies. The farmer of jokes was a different guy altogether, he thought, one who would invite a man into the farmhouse to eat dinner and meet his comely young daughter. He was friendly at first but had a low tolerance for strangers' hijinks.)

No farmer of any type appeared. The ostrich stretched his long neck toward Mark.

(His neck? Her neck? How could you tell?)

"Hey, friend," Mark said. "We're just having car trouble. As soon as someone gets here to help us, we'll be on our way."

The ostrich glared at him. Or perhaps he was glaring at the ostrich. He thought of a line he'd seen on an inspirational poster. *We do not see things as they are, but as we are.* Something like that.

Perhaps he was the angry one, defending his territory. His boyfriend. His piece-of-shit car. His right to break down in the middle of nowhere next to this ostrich's fence.

Mark could feel sweat running down his sides. They were going to get burnt for sure. It hadn't occurred to him to pack sunblock. (They were going to his mother's. She had at least six different types of sunblock in her bathroom cabinet.)

"Stay away from him," Mark's boyfriend said, though Mark had no intention of going anywhere near the ostrich. Did he look like someone who was trying to get his eyes pecked out?

He was standing by the side of the road in a $200 pair of jeans with a cell phone and designer sunglasses from Italy in one hand.

Perversely, though, he took a step closer to the fence. "Maybe he'd like a potato chip," he said.

Mark's boyfriend had bought a bag of Lay's at a gas station earlier in the day. Mark leaned in the open window of the car and pulled out the chips.

His boyfriend's face was turning red. "Stop it! He can't eat that."

Even the ostrich looked like he thought Mark had gone too far. "Sorry," Mark muttered. He handed his boyfriend the bag.

By the time they arrived at Mark's mother's house, they were out more than five hundred dollars, between the car repairs and the ad hoc hotel stay.

If they'd known what was going to happen, they agreed, they would have skipped the sunset cruise. They were going to have to pinch pennies for a while.

The night of the cruise, though, they got dressed up and sat waiting in the living room. Mark's mother came downstairs in a sleeveless A-line party dress and low heels with straps across the ankles.

They all drove down to the dock. They were a few minutes early. In line, as they were waiting to board the ship, Mark found himself standing next to a large man who smelled like coconut suntan lotion. The sun was shining on the water. Mark's mother put her hand on his arm and said, "I'm so happy."

In her early twenties, his mother had been in a bad car accident. The doctors told her that she would never be able to have children. She was forty-one when she unexpectedly got pregnant with him (and became convinced, for at least a couple of months, that she was going through menopause). He had only seen his father a handful of times.

Mark had driven down to Florida. His boyfriend took a different route on the way home, so Mark knew they wouldn't pass the ostrich farm.

Often, on the return trip, Mark found himself looking out the window. They were listening to a book on tape. A few years earlier, he had been living on the opposite coast, alone, and had impulsively applied for a job transfer to be closer to his mother. Now here he was, sailing through an indifferent landscape with his boyfriend at his side, on the lookout for wildlife.

That weekend, on the boat, a woman claimed to have seen a pair of dolphins break the surface of the water. He hadn't seen them himself, but who knew? There were certain times in life, he thought, when any surprising thing seemed possible.

Rats (10.24.2016: p. 67)

She spent the night in a hotel room near LAX. After a few days, she could feel at home in a strange place, but there wasn't going to be enough time. She slept poorly. In the middle of the night, the person in the room overhead began shuffling around or moving something back and forth across the floor. She could just hear scratching sounds, as if the walls were filled with rats. On the plane, she'd read an issue of *The New Yorker* with a cartoon she couldn't make sense of—a sketch of a bull with a sad expression wearing a dress shirt and tie with a button pinned to his jacket that said, "Ask me about mazes." She couldn't stop thinking about scientific research, the rats and mice who were set down in one place and timed as they scurried around, sniffing out treats. Someone was always tracking your progress. Scratch, scratch.

In the morning, before she went downstairs to catch the shuttle, she made coffee in the room. She was on the seventh floor of the hotel. Outside, it was overcast. The Styrofoam cup was warm against her hands. From the window, she could see planes descending toward the airport. All that was visible, at first, was a tiny glittering white light, and then behind it a faint outline as the plane grew closer: a recognizable shape emerging through the clouds.

Acknowledgments

Grateful acknowledgment is made to the editors of the following publications in which these stories first appeared, sometimes in slightly different form:

Blue Lake Review: "Armie"

Clementine Unbound: "Elise in Austria"

Every Pigeon: "Role-Play"

Funicular Magazine: "Rats (10.24.2016: p. 67)"

Litro: "Elise in Croatia"

Random Sample Review: "From a Distance, It Always Sounds Like Begging"

Route 7 Review: "Shame"

Waypoints: "Elise in Italy"